# Rose Gold
## and Friends

Published in the UK by Scholastic Children's Books, 2020
Euston House, 24 Eversholt Street, London, NW1 1DB, UK
A division of Scholastic Limited.

London – New York – Toronto – Sydney – Auckland
Mexico City – New Delhi – Hong Kong

Text © Alice Hemming 2020
Cover characters and inisde Illustrations by Dan Crisp in the style of
Kerry LaRue © Scholastic, 2020

The right of Alice Hemming to be identified as the author of this work has
been asserted by her under the Copyright, Designs and Patents Act 1988.

ISBN 978 1407 19669 5

A CIP catalogue record for this book is available from the British Library.

Printed by CPI Group (UK) Ltd, Croydon, CR0 4YY
Papers used by Scholastic Children's Books are made
from wood grown in sustainable forests.

1 3 5 7 9 10 8 6 4 2

www.scholastic.co.uk

For Kefira and Taliya

# Rose Gold
## and Friends

# Amber's Mystery Sleepover

## ALICE HEMMING

SCHOLASTIC

# Chapter 1

## Back Together

"Thank you for having us, Mrs Beau," said Rose shyly to Amber's mum.

"Do call me Monisha. And it's lovely to have you here. What with four girls, two boys, a dog, and a coop full of chickens, there's always room for a few more!"

Rose, Yasmeen and Oralie had just

arrived at Amber's house, where they were staying for a few nights. Amber and her mum, who looked like an older version of Amber with shorter hair, were giving them a tour.

"Your house is lovely!" said Rose, gazing around appreciatively.

"It is as big as BigToes Hall! And as beautiful!" agreed Oralie.

The friends had met at Camp Bickrose (which they called Camp BigToes) during the summer. They got on so well that they met up again at Yasmeen's house for the Christmas holidays and now at Amber's during February half term.

"It might be big and beautiful but there is *nothing* to do here!" said Amber. "That's one reason I went to summer camp. And to get away from my brothers and sisters! Speaking of which, my little sister Leena is excited about meeting you all." Amber pointed to a little girl hiding behind Monisha. Leena looked like a younger version of Amber with longer hair. "This is my dolly," she said, holding out a tatty fabric doll.

"Your doll is very pretty," said Yasmeen, kindly.

"Would you like to play?" asked Leena.

Monisha stepped in. "Yasmeen will play later. Leena, would you like to help me decorate some yummy biscuits?"

Leena nodded

and smiled as Monisha whisked her away. Amber mouthed, "Thank you."

"She would want to play all day otherwise," Amber explained to the others. "My other brothers and sisters are bigger. Two are away at university. Sara and Omesh are upstairs. They are teenagers."

She beckoned the girls through the hallway. "Come on, let me show you the Snug, where we're going to sleep!"

The Snug was a huge family room at the back of the house with glass doors facing the garden. There was a big TV, computer, games, sofa and some colourful beanbags. Four camp beds were already set up on the floor but there was still space around them. The girls had all brought sleeping bags and pillows. Rose started to unroll hers on the bed in the left-hand corner. "Let's sleep on the same sides as we did at camp and at Yasmeen's," suggested Rose.

"Good plan," said Yasmeen, putting her sleeping bag on one of the beds on the right side of the room.

There was a sign balanced on an art easel near the glass doors. At the top, it read *Welcome to Camp BigBeau* (Beau was Amber's surname). Oralie ran over to take a look. "Oh look, you've even made a timetable like we had at camp!" she said.

**"Monday: midnight feast, film.**
**Tuesday: chocolate, film.**
**Wednesday: pizza, film.**
**Thurday: pizza, film.**
**Friday: home :( :("**

Amber laughed. "It's only a joke,

though. We can do whatever we like!"

On the sofa was what looked like a fluffy white cushion with eyes. It turned out to be a dog, white but with golden patches on her back and golden ears, and a pink tongue. She yapped excitedly. Rose sat down and began stroking soothingly and Amber joined her on the other side. "This is Fluffikins."

"What is she?" asked Yasmeen.

"She is a big fluffball. She is lovely but lately, she's been getting a bit lazy. Mum says we're going to put her on a diet."

"I meant what breed?" asked Yasmeen, joining them on the sofa.

"She is a Pomeranian. A Pom. Leena says she looks like a pompom too! Leena is the one who called her Fluffikins, because she is the fluffiest thing we've ever seen."

"Close your eyes!" said Oralie, suddenly. The girls all closed their eyes. They could hear Oralie rummaging about in her bag.

"Can we open them yet?" asked Amber after a few moments.

"Ten more seconds," said Oralie. There was the sound of a zip. "Open your eyes now!"

Oralie stood in a bright white fluffy onesie with ears and a tail. "*Now* what is the fluffiest thing you've ever seen?"

The girls laughed. Oralie took a running jump over her camp bed to join them on the sofa. They stroked Oralie's arms.

"You may actually be fluffier than Fluffikins, now," said Amber.

Amber picked up Fluffikins and placed her on Oralie's lap. "What do you think?" she asked the dog.

Fluffikins didn't look as if she minded; she was just happy to have a fuss made of her. The girls stroked and petted her, and Fluffikins lapped up all the attention.

"Oralie has the right idea – I'm going to get into my onesie too," said Rose, leaping up. The others followed and they were soon in their onesies, even though it was only three p.m..

"Ooh, let's do our Treasure Box rhyme!" said Amber, excitedly. Pushing up their sleeves to reveal their shiny bracelets, they stood in a circle, crossed their arms and held hands. Each of their bracelets matched their own precious metal: Rose Gold, Yasmeen Silver, Amber Beau and Oralie Sands. They chanted together:

*"Make new friends but keep the old,*
*Amber, Silver, Rose and Gold."*

Rose pulled her friends back on to the sofa. They sat all squished up, with Fluffikins snuggling in the middle. "It's so good to be back together!"

"What shall we do tonight?" asked Amber.

Oralie stroked her chin and looked over at the easel. "How about ..."

All the girls looked at her expectantly. She was good at original ideas.

"... a pizza and a film?"

They fell back on the cushions, laughing. Hanging out together,

watching their favourite films and wearing onesies all week. This was going to be the Best. Half term. EVER!

# Chapter 2

## Not Quite Midnight

That night, there was no way the girls were going straight to sleep after the film. They had far too much to catch up on. It had been ages since they'd seen one another. They had been in touch over email, though, and had been planning a Midnight Feast.

"Did everyone bring something?" asked Amber

The girls nodded and ran to their bags. Yasmeen produced a packet of popcorn, Rose had biscuits and Amber planned to raid the fridge for cheese.

"Guess what I've brought," said Oralie, throwing clothes out of her bag in an attempt to find the hidden stash.

"TOMATO KETCHUP CRISPS?" they all guessed together. Oralie had discovered that they were the girls' favourite crisps at camp. Oralie laughed and pulled out a large plastic multipack. "Twelve packets. Should be enough for one week!" She threw the crisps on to the tasty-looking pile of food.

"Let's save it all until everyone is asleep," said Amber.

"What shall we do until then?" asked Rose.

"Let's share any news and secrets we've been saving up."

Oralie clapped her hands together. "I've got something I've been bursting to tell you all."

Amber smiled. "Does it have anything to do with puppies, by any chance?" Oralie was obsessed with her new puppy.

"No, not this time! This is *new* news. I've decided to become a detective! I have this amazing book that tells you how to write secret notes, solve codes and identify suspects – look!" Oralie fished a blue book out of her bag called *How to be a Top Detective*. It had a picture of a man with a magnifying glass on the front.

Rose flicked through the pages. "Could you could teach us?"

"Ooh yes, we could be a team of detectives, solving mysteries," said

Yasmeen.

"We could help people solve crimes. Let's start tomorrow! I've got a magnifying glass, a special notebook, a fingerprint set..." Oralie began unpacking all sorts of detective equipment.

Amber laughed and put her hand over Oralie's to stop her for a moment. "We won't find any crimes here in Mynton. Nothing ever happens around here. The biggest drama we ever had was when Mr

Sullivan put some stickers on his wheelie bins. The neighbour across the road complained that they were too colourful!"

Oralie looked disappointed. "Wheelie bin stickers? Really?"

"Yes. Like I said – mega dull."

"Well you never know. Sometimes, in the films, mysteries happen just as the detectives arrive," said Oralie. She tucked her notebook into her onesie pocket.

Amber sat up in bed. "My turn next! I'm not sure if I am supposed to tell you this or not... I mean no one said to keep it a secret... But we normally have fireworks here in the garden for Diwali. Some people from the village come along. Mum said that this year, we can do it all again in February so that you can watch them too!"

"Yay! It can be our grand finale!"

said Yasmeen. "This is going to be such a good week!"

"What about Fluffikins?" wondered Oralie, cuddling the dog.

"What do you mean?" asked Amber.

"She's in the circle. She needs to share a secret too!"

"Fluffikins hasn't got any secrets," said Amber. "She's too busy eating and sleeping."

"Speaking of eating... Is it time for our midnight feast, yet?" asked Yasmeen.

"Not yet. It's 10.16 p.m.," said Amber.

"I don't know if I can wait another hour and a half for my crisps," said Oralie.

Yasmeen yawned. "And I'm getting tired."

There was a knock at the door. Amber's mum opened the door and poked her head in. "Can I still hear

voices in there, girls? Let me guess –
you're planning a midnight feast?"

The girls nodded. Rumbled. And they
thought they'd been so quiet.

"Midnight seems a little late. You won't
be able to open your eyes tomorrow.
How about we have a 10.30pm feast?"
The girls agreed, so Monisha brought in
a picnic blanket and spread it
out on the floor by the

camp beds. They opened their stash of food and each had a mug of milk, too. By the time they were halfway through the feast, the girls were all yawning.

"I'm so sleepy! I'm ready for bed now," said Yasmeen.

"I'm so excited, I feel like I could stay up all night!" cried Oralie.

Monisha cleared the

blankets away and took Fluffikins to her bed in the kitchen. The girls made their way back to their camp beds. They snuggled down into their cosy sleeping bags.

"Everyone comfy?" checked Amber.

"Yes, snug as a bug in a rug!" said Yasmeen.

"You're not feeling too homesick are you, Rose?"

At summer camp, Rose had missed her dog, Wriggly. But right now she seemed very happy. "I won't be homesick this week. I know Wriggly is happy because he is on holiday with my mum and dad and being very spoiled. Anyway, if I need a dog to stroke, then there's always Fluffikins!"

Amber turned out the last light. "Goodnight, everyone."

The girls all moved into comfy sleeping

positions, apart from Oralie, who yelped and jumped up. "Aargh! NO WAY! I thought Fluffikins was in here but it was just a cushion."

"Fluffikins is asleep in the kitchen," said Amber.

"Night, then," said Rose. Yasmeen yawned.

Everything was silent for a few moments.

Oralie giggled. "Do you ever have that thing where everything goes suddenly quiet and it makes you want to say something?"

"No! Go to sleep!"

Oralie giggled.

"GO TO SLEEP, ORALIE!"

"OK – I'm going to sleep now. Night night."

"Night night."

# Chapter 3

## Walkies

Amber was the first one up. She pulled open the long curtains that covered the glass doors and sunlight filled the room.

"Too bright," moaned Oralie from deep inside her sleeping bag.

Yasmeen sat up and threw a cushion at her. "You were the one who wanted to talk all night – now you have to get up!"

They all threw cushions at Oralie until she emerged, rubbing her eyes.

"Come on!" cried Amber. "You have to get up. There is too much to do! Films to watch! Pizza to eat!"

"Pancakes for breakfast!" called Monisha from the kitchen.

The girls all sniffed the air. The smell of fried batter enticed them into the kitchen.

Amber's mum had made a great big stack of American-style pancakes that were perfectly round and fluffy and delicious. She served them with a bowl of fruit salad and offered syrup or chocolate spread. Leena was already tucking into hers at the table and the older children wandered in and out. Fluffikins had her own breakfast in the corner.

"What do you like on yours?" Monisha asked Oralie.

Oralie looked at the wonderful array. "Erm, a bit of everything, please!"

"This is the best breakfast ever!" said Rose as they all tucked in to their amazing pancakes.

Monisha poured herself a cup of coffee. "Are you girls planning to go outside at all today?"

Amber scratched her head, pretending to think. "Outside? Hmmm. Our timetable says pizza, midnight feasts and films. There is no mention of outside! We were planning to stay in our onesies all week!"

Monisha looked disappointed. "Oh. I was hoping you could take Fluffikins for a walk. She needs her exercise."

Amber laughed. "Only joking, Mum. Of course we'll take Fluffikins out."

"Lets stay in our onesies anyway. We can put our coats over the top," suggested Oralie.

The others giggled. "Good plan!" said Yasmeen, and they all adopted the onesie, jacket and trainers look. It was actually quite practical for the chilly February day.

Fluffikins seemed quite enthusiastic about a walk when Amber dangled her lead. She yapped, ran around in small circles and enjoyed some petting and stroking. But by the time they'd got to the bottom of Amber's long driveway, Fluffikins had run out of puff and was lagging behind the girls.

From Amber's house, they had to turn right, walk a little way along, and then it was a short walk up a steepish hill to the village. At the bottom of the hill,

Fluffikins sat down and turned her big black eyes towards Amber.

"Oh, Fluffikins, you are such a princess!" Amber reached down and scooped her up.

"Are you actually carrying your pooch up this hill?" asked Oralie.

"Yes! Look what happens if I put her down." After a few paces, Amber put Fluffikins down on her feet. She sat down on her bottom straightaway and looked up at the girls questioningly. Amber gently pulled the lead but Fluffikins pulled back. She wasn't going to climb the hill.

They giggled. Amber picked her up again.

"Come on then, Fluffikins – let's get you up this hill."

Halfway up the hill, a red car pulled up alongside them. Amber clearly recognized the driver straight way. "Hello, Miss Scott," she said.

Miss Scott wound down her window. "Just checking everything is OK. I saw you picking up your dog. Is she poorly? Do you need a lift to the vets?"

"No," said Amber, smiling awkwardly. "She just isn't very keen on hills."

"Ah ... I understand! See you after half term." Miss Scott buzzed the window back up and drove away.

"That was my teacher! She probably thinks I carry Fluffikins everywhere now." Amber put Fluffikins back on the ground. "Come on, you can walk."

Fluffikins seemed to be happy now that they were back on level ground and she trotted along obediently behind the girls.

As they walked up into the village, Amber gestured to the right and left at anything interesting. "So, the grand tour. This shouldn't take too long. This is where nothing happens on a Monday, this is where nothing happens on a Tuesday, this is where nothing happens on a Wed—"

They passed a tall woman in a long coat. She stopped to stroke the dog. "Hello, Amber. Hello, Fluffikins."

"Hello, Reverend," said Amber.

She smiled and waved goodbye.

"Do you know everyone here?" whispered Rose.

"Pretty much," said Amber, with a giggle.

Although it was only February, the sun was out and it was warm enough to play in the park. The girls went on the swings and the roundabout. The trees were mainly bare of leaves but the sky was blue and the winter sun shone on the rooftops. Rose always had an eye out for interesting colour combinations. "Look, I can see all the colours of our bracelets," she called, as she swung up high.

They popped into the post office opposite the park and bought a magazine. It had a free toy aeroplane attached and they spend a happy twenty minutes launching it from the top of the climbing frame.

After a while Amber checked her

watch. "I told Mum we'd be back by eleven. We'd better start heading back down the hill."

When they were nearly back at Amber's house they heard a voice calling from behind some bushes. "Snowball! Snowball!"

Fluffikins' ears pricked up and she dashed off, faster than the girls had seen her move before. She raced around the hedge and up the driveway next to Amber's house.

"Where's she going?" asked Yasmeen.

"It's OK — she's just off to see Mrs Mack," said Amber.

They followed Fluffikins' path around the hedge and saw her jumping up at Amber's neighbour's knees. Mrs Mack had curly black hair, a flowery scarf and bright turquoise slippers. She put her watering can down at her feet and reached into her sleeveless jacket. She brought out a handful of dog treats for Fluffikins, who chewed them up gratefully.

"Er, Mum says we're not supposed to be giving her treats between meals," said Amber. "She's been putting on a bit of weight."

"Nonsense!" said Mrs Mack, handing Fluffikins another treat. "It's all fluff, isn't it, Snowball?"

Fluffikins gobbled up the treat happily.

"Why do you call her Snowball? Her name is Fluffikins," said Oralie.

"I can never seem to remember that. I had a little dog called Snowball once, a long time ago. He was such a good dog. He looked a lot like this one here."

She leaned down and patted Fluffikins on the head. "What about you, girls? Would you like to come in for a glass of juice and some of my lemon and poppyseed biscuits?"

"Thank you very much but we'd better go, Mrs Mack, otherwise my mum will wonder where we are," said Amber.

Mrs Mack straightened up.

"No problem. Have a lovely day. Don't be strangers now, will you?"

The girls nodded and made their way back to Amber's house. They raced in from their walk with bright eyes and flushed faces. More delicious smells – like baked bread – were coming from the kitchen.

Amber's mum greeted them at the door and made them leave their trainers and coats in the porch. Fluffikins seemed relieved to be home and sat on one of Amber's trainers, gently panting.

"I was right! That outing did you all good. Now who's for hot chocolate?"

"Yes please!"

"With marshmallows?"

"YES PLEASE!"

"Coming right up," said Monisha.

The walk had given the girls new energy and after the hot chocolate, they decided to play in the garden. The sun was still strong and the ground was dry. Some snowdrops were peeping out under the trees near where the chickens were pecking about. At the back of Amber's garden were a number of big, older trees. Together, they leaned branches against the trunks and pegged sheets over them. After an hour or so, they had built a den big enough for all four girls to lie on their backs. They filled it with mats, blankets and cushions and it was super cosy.

"It's a shame it's not summer. We could have slept out here," said Amber.

"I am happier sleeping inside. You never know what's about," said Rose.

At that moment, someone lifted the sheet and the girls all screamed.

It was just Monisha. "Sorry, I didn't mean to alarm you. Are you ready for lunch?"

"Can we eat out here? Pleeeeease?" begged Amber.

So Monisha obliged and brought trays of food out to them — sandwiches, samosas and cruchy vegetable sticks.

Once finished, they took their plates back inside. Monisha was smiling, as usual, but she wore a slightly worried expression too.

"I have been looking for Fluffikins. She hasn't been out in the garden with you, has she?"

"No – I'd have heard her chasing the chickens," said Amber.

Monisha's smile vanished, leaving just the worry.

"I can't find her anywhere. We've looked all round the house and outside. Fluffikins is *missing*!"

# Chapter 4

## Finding Fluffikins

"What do you mean, missing?" asked
Amber.

"We've checked all her usual favourite
spots but she seems to have completely
disappeared," said Monisha.

"She came in with us after the walk,"
said Rose.

"Yes, but maybe I forgot to close the

door and she ran out in all the hubbub."
Monisha wrung her hands together. "I'm
so worried that something may have
happened."

"Don't worry. I'm sure she will turn
up," said Yasmeen. "Shall we check the
house and gardens again?"

The girls all nodded.

"Thank you. I'll drive up to the vet's
with Leena. If Fluffikins was hurt, then
someone might have taken her there."

The girls checked the house, all the
cupboards, sheds, greenhouse and their
homemade tent but there was no sign of
her. Monisha and Leena returned from
the vets empty handed. Fluffikins seemed
to have completely vanished.

Leena was in tears and Amber was
getting upset, too. "What are we going
to do?" she cried.

Yasmeen put her arm around Amber and handed Leena a tissue.

Oralie went to get her detective book. "There's something in here that might give us a clue…"

Rose tapped Monisha gently on the shoulder. "Excuse me, but do you have an up-to-date photo of Fluffikins?"

"Yes, I've got absolutely loads. Why?"

"I was thinking we could make a poster to say she's missing."

"What a good idea. OK, you sit here and flick through these. See which one you think is best."

Rose and Amber squeezed on to the chair at the computer desk in the Snug and Yasmeen stood behind them.

There were loads of pictures of Fluffikins. One particularly good one showed her stretched out on her back on a sun lounger. "That was on holiday. She didn't like getting too hot," explained Amber.

"Choose a close up one so that people can see her clearly," called Oralie, still reading through her detective book.

The girls picked a close-up shot where Fluffikins was looking directly into the camera. "This one is perfect. You can see that her ears are a slightly different colour to the rest of her body. She also has that ginger patch on her back," said Rose.

"Mum! We've chosen one!" called Amber.

"Great. Now do you know how to drop that picture into a document and make a poster?" asked Monisha.

"I think so," said Yasmeen. Together, the girls worked to choose some good lettering and to get the wording right.

### MISSING
*Beloved pet.*
*Answers to the name of Fluffikins.*
*Last seen on Tuesday morning. Please check your sheds and garages in case she's locked in somewhere.*

They added Monisha's phone number at

the bottom and printed off twenty copies.

"Do you want us to go and put these up around the village?" asked Rose.

"Yes, please, girls," said Monisha, handing them some sticky tape. "Put one on each lamppost going up the hill, one by the church, and if you check with the post office, I'm sure they'll let you put one on their notice board."

The girls left straight away, taking exactly the same route they had that morning.

Amber wasn't her usual springy self. "I feel a bit better now that we're doing something but I'm still worried. It's just not like Fluffikins to go missing."

"Don't worry," said Yasmeen.

"She'll be OK," said Rose, squeezing her friend's hand. She knew how she would feel if Wriggly went missing.

Oralie put an arm around her. "I'm sure there's a reasonable explanation. I saw this film once where a dog climbed inside a truck without the owner knowing. They drove four hundred miles away and the dog still made it back to his family."

Amber's mouth dropped open. "What? I don't want Fluffikins to end up four hundred miles away!"

"I'm not saying she will, but she could have jumped in a van or something and the driver wouldn't necessarily notice."

"She's chipped, isn't she? That means if anyone finds her and takes her to a vets or a rescue centre then they'll trace her straight back to you," said Yasmeen.

That seemed to make Amber feel a bit better and they carried on putting up posters, looking behind hedges and fences as they went. They were attaching the final poster to the lamppost outside Mrs Mack's house, when Amber spotted her looking out of the window. She shuffled out into the street in her slippers.

"What's on the posters, girls?"

Yasmeen explained and Mrs Mack read the poster, shaking her head sadly. "Poor Snowball. Such a pretty dog. With such soft fur. And a calm personality. I can see why someone would take her."

Amber's face fell. "Take her? You think someone's *stolen* Fluffikins?"

# Chapter 5

## Dog Detectives

Back in the Snug, Oralie picked up her
notebook and a pencil and stood chewing
the end for a second. Then she raised
a hand. "We need a proper criminal
investigation."

"What does that mean?" asked Rose.

"I'll show you." She turned to Amber.
"Do you have any sticky notes? Paper?

Pens? And a big piece of paper to glue it all on?"

Amber found everything in the desk and passed them to Oralie. "What do we need those for?"

"We are going to create a *crime wall*. It's what real detectives do."

"I'm not sure about sticking stuff to the wall. I don't think my parents would be too happy," said Amber.

"We could use the easel," suggested Yasmeen.

Oralie removed the *Camp BickBeau* sign from the easel and attached a blank sheet of paper with sticky tape. At the top of the paper she wrote:

THE DISAPPEARANCE
OF FLUFFIKINS:
CASE OPEN

"We need to put up everything we know on this crime wall ... or crime board. Photos, maps, pictures. And link stuff with lines. It's like a big puzzle. When we see it all up here together, the answer will jump out at us."

"And we'll find Fluffikins?" asked Amber.

"That's right." Oralie took one of the lost dog posters and carefully cut out the picture of Fluffikins, which she glued to the centre of the board. Amber and Yasmeen printed out maps and pictures to stick on. Rose was good at drawing, so she drew pictures of anything they couldn't find online.

Oralie shouted out questions as they went along.

"Where was Fluffikins the last time we saw her?"

"Who was the last person apart from us to see Fluffikins?

Some of the questions were a bit strange.

"What's the vicar called? What about your teacher?"

"Reverend Norris. And Miss Scott. But they wouldn't take Fluffikins!" cried Amber.

"Perhaps, but we have to look at the whole picture before we decide. Anything might give us a clue," said Oralie.

Oralie worked hard. When the others stopped for biscuits, she ate hers standing up by the easel. Then she stopped in front of the board with one hand over her mouth. "Look! I've discovered something."

Amber, Rose and Yasmeen obligingly

came over and sat in front of the
easel. Oralie stood to the side so that
they could all see the crime board.
The photograph of Fluffikins was now
surrounded by a mass of sticky notes and
pen-drawn lines. To the left was a map
of the village.

Oralie seemed excited. "What do
you see? What stands out?"

Yasmeen peered

closely. "I don't mean to be rude but that just looks like ... a big squiggle."

"It might look like a squiggle but we need all these lines and pictures to make the links. Often in dognapping – when someone steals a dog – the dognapper was the last person to see the dog. And *this* was the last person – apart from us – to see Fluffikins."

Oralie tapped her pen on a stick figure wearing a flowery scarf and turquoise slippers. Rose had drawn a good likeness. It was Mrs Mack, Amber's next-door neighbour. Oralie stood back. "Now do you see?"

The others shook their heads.

Oralie paused dramatically. "All the evidence suggests that Fluffikins *has* been stolen. Stolen by Mrs Mack!"

# Chapter 6

## Mrs Mack

"Mrs Mack?" cried Amber, shocked. "No. She wouldn't do a thing like that. She's a nice person."

"A bit lonely, maybe," said Yasmeen.

"And she loves Fluffikins," added Rose.

"Exactly," said Oralie. "That is her *motive*. Her reason for the dognap."

She tapped another area of the crime

wall where *motive* was underlined. Underneath, it read:

To take Fluffikins (aka Snowball) as a companion.

"*And* she was the last person to see her *and* she was behaving oddly *and* she is in the perfect location. She could just lean over the fence and grab her any time she wanted. That's called *opportunity*." Oralie tapped the crime wall again and continued.

"*And* she acted pretty strangely when we reported Fluffikins missing. Nobody even considered that someone had stolen Fluffikins, but Mrs Mack put the idea in our heads."

"I'm not sure," said Yasmeen. "We can't just go round accusing people."

Oralie nodded gravely. "Exactly. And that is why we are going straight outside to gather some *evidence*."

# Chapter 7

## Gathering Evidence

Out in Amber's garden, Oralie sat at the top of the garden slide with her legs resting on the wavy blue plastic. Amber stood behind her, holding a pair of binoculars, with Rose on the step behind. Yasmeen had refused to climb the ladder and stood to the side of the slide.

Amber looked through her binoculars over the fence into Mrs Mack's garden. "What am I looking for?" she asked.

Oralie tapped her notebook. "We are here to gather *evidence*. Like Yasmeen said, we can't just go around accusing people. Proper facts are needed."

"But I'm really not sure that pointing binoculars over the fence is a good idea," called Yasmeen from the bottom of the slide.

Oralie shrugged. "We could have made

a periscope but there wasn't time."

"Aren't we committing a crime by staring at Mrs Mack in her own house? Isn't that a different crime? Like stalking or something?" called Yasmeen.

"Yes, I don't know how happy my parents are going to be about this," said Amber.

"They will be really happy when we find Fluffikins though, won't they?" said Rose, trying to stand on her tiptoes to look with Amber.

"Can you see anything?" Oralie asked Amber.

Amber looked up and down the garden. "Nothing. Just grass. And pretty flowers. Mrs Mack likes gardening."

"But anything that looks like *evidence*?"

Amber continued to scan up and down. "No. Nothing. Oh, hang on a minute, there is something yellow in the flowerbed. A tennis ball."

"A tennis ball!" cried Oralie, excitedly. "That could be evidence. I'm going to write it down."

"Evidence of what?" asked Rose.

"It might be to entertain Fluffikins when Mrs Mack lets her out. She's probably planning to walk her at night when nobody sees her. Anything else, Amber?"

Amber looked back down Mrs Mack's garden, towards the house.

"I can see Mrs Mack!" cried Amber. "She's in the kitchen!"

"You really shouldn't be looking at someone in her house. That's an invasion of privacy," said Yasmeen.

But Amber kept her binoculars trained on the house. "Just for a second."

"What's she doing?" asked Oralie.

"I think she's talking to someone, but I can't see anyone else there."

"No other *person* anyway," said Oralie.

"Now she's opening a cupboard and putting something inside—"

"What?" cried Rose.

Amber peered. "I'm not sure... It might be a dog's bowl!"

"EVIDENCE!" shrieked Oralie.

"I think she saw me!" Amber ducked down, nearly falling off the slide and sending Oralie shooting down to the bottom and straight into Yasmeen.

It took them a few moments to untangle themselves but Oralie stood up with purpose. "We need to go over there right now and knock on the door!"

"Let's do it!" said Amber, linking her arm through Oralie's.

"O...K," said Rose, slightly more

reluctantly.

"I still think this is a bad idea," said Yasmeen, but she followed the others anyway.

# Chapter 8

## Accused!

Mrs Mack's door was the same bright turquoise colour as her slippers, with two rectangular panels of swirly glass and a black doorknocker in the shape of a fox in the middle. A pretty flowering basket hung to the right.

All four girls stood on the steps and stared at the knocker. Even Oralie seemed slightly less enthusiastic about confronting Mrs Mack now that they were actually there. But she took a deep breath, lifted the fox, and knocked.

Mrs Mack opened the door with a wide smile. "Hello, girls! Back already? Did you find Snowball?"

Amber looked at her shoes. "No. That's what ... erm ... we have come to ask you about..."

"Well, do come in and have some of my lemon and poppyseed biscuits." Mrs Mack led them through into the kitchen. She put a plate of her homemade biscuits and a jug of orange squash on the table. Amber, Yasmeen and Rose stood nibbling the biscuits politely and Oralie backed towards the cupboard where they'd seen the dog food.

Mrs Mack looked around and then

quickly closed the door to the hall. Oralie brought her notebook and scribbled in it.

"What are you writing, dear?" asked Mrs Mack.

Oralie tapped her pen on her notebook. "Evidence!" she cried, suddenly. "Tell me – why did you close the door just then?"

Mrs Mack looked puzzled. "I thought there was a bit of a draught."

"Ha!" cried Oralie, loudly. "Are you sure you're not hiding something?"

The other girls looked at their shoes.

Mrs Mack sat down and picked up a biscuit. "No, dear. I find that there are quite a lot of draughts at this time of year—"

"So what were you doing in here?" Oralie flung open the door of the kitchen cupboard behind her. The girls all stared and Mrs Mack put her hands over her mouth. The cupboard was filled from top to bottom with packets and tins of dog food, dog treats and dog toys.

Amber gasped.

"Oh dear," said Mrs Mack.

"Where are you hiding Fluffikins?" blurted Oralie.

"Oh no, I wouldn't take Snowball," said Mrs Mack. "I'm very fond of her and her lovely family. But she has been so hungry lately..."

There was a loud knock at the door.

"I'd better get that," said Mrs Mack, and she shuffled off to answer it.

"I don't think she's done anything wrong," whispered Yasmeen.

"I still think she's hiding something," said Oralie, but she didn't sound too sure.

Mrs Mack came back into the kitchen with Amber's older sister, Sara.

"Mum just called. She's found Fluffikins."

"Oh," said Oralie.

Amber's face broke into a smile. "Where?"

"She's at the vet's," said Sara.

Amber went pale. "What's wrong with her?"

"Mum didn't say. Just that we should all get up there straight away. But I don't think it's anything too serious."

Yasmeen turned to Mrs Mack. "So if Fluffikins is at the vet's, then..."

Mrs Mack spread out her hands. "Then she's not here. That's what I've been trying to tell you all."

Oralie looked at the door and then back at Mrs Mack "But the evidence ... the motive..."

Mrs Mack shrugged. "It was nothing to do with me, my dear."

# Chapter 9

## Surprise!

The bell on the door jangled as Amber
rushed in to the vet's, with the others
close behind. She raced up to the man
at the reception desk. "We're looking for
Fluffikins?"

He tapped on the keyboard and
glanced at the screen. "Surname?"

"Beau."

"Fluffikins Beau... Consulting room three."

They all ran through the waiting area, past a woman with a huge white rabbit in a pet carrier. They knocked on the door of room three and there was Fluffikins, standing up on the examination table, eyes bright and tail wagging. Her mouth was open and she

was panting gently. She looked fluffy and rounded and pretty much the same as she had the last time they saw her. When she saw Amber, she yapped and tried to run off the side; the vet had to hold her back.

Amber laughed and went straight over to stroke her. "She looks absolutely fine!" she said. "I was so worried when you got us here. Is everything OK?"

Monisha smiled a wide smile. "Everything is absolutely OK. Fluffikins and her puppies are going to be just fine."

"Puppies?"

"Yes! Fluffikins is carrying puppies and they are due to be born..."

"...Any day now!" said the vet.

"I can't believe we didn't notice," said Monisha. "That explains why she has been so slow recently. She's not lazy at all!"

The vet nodded. "You may have found she has been a lot hungrier, too."
The girls looked guiltily at one another.

"We were planning for her to have puppies but didn't realize it had happened yet," said Monisha.

"A Pomeranian's fur can hide a lot," said the vet. "You're not the first dog owner who has missed a pregnancy."

"I figured it out the minute I found her. She was hiding under the clothes in the ironing basket in the airing cupboard," said Monisha. "That's when I knew."

"Yes, dogs have a nesting instinct when they are soon to have puppies. They like to go somewhere quiet, warm and dark, to get away from any hustle and bustle," said the vet.

Amber laughed. "There's always a lot of hustle and bustle at our house."

"Poor Fluffikins. We'll give you a bit of peace and quiet now," said Yasmeen.

"Yes, we need to look after her," said Monisha.

"Come on, let's get you home."

The next day went in a blur. There were more films and pizzas, of course, and they all wrote a letter to Mrs Mack to say sorry and to explain about the puppies. Rose even drew a good likeness of Fluffikins on the envelope.

That afternoon, Monisha announced that Fluffikins was almost ready to have the puppies. She was busy making sure that Fluffikins was well-looked after, so Amber's big brother, Omesh, got the girls their dinner.

At bedtime, Monisha said, "Get a good night's sleep tonight. It looks like there will be puppies by the morning!"

But the girls couldn't get to sleep at all.

"I'm so worried about Fluffikins," said Amber.

"She'll be fine," said Yasmeen.

"I'm so excited to see the puppies!" added Rose.

"I wonder if they'll be as fluffy as Fluffikins." Oralie smiled.

At just after eleven o'clock, Monisha opened the door to the Snug.

"I thought you'd still be awake! I've got something to show you all..."

"Puppies!" cried the girls. They zipped up their onesies and followed Monisha upstairs to the guestroom. In a snug-

looking dog bed, Fluffikins lay with her two new puppies, who were feeding happily. One was white and one was ginger.

"She looks so proud!" said Amber, who looked proud herself.

"She's going to be a good mother," agreed Monisha.

"Why are there only two puppies? I thought dogs had lots," said Yasmeen.

"It's normal for a Pomeranian to have a small litter. That's another reason we didn't spot that she was having them," explained Monisha.

"They are so cute! But they look like hamsters! I thought they'd be fluffy!" said Oralie.

Monisha shook her head. "It takes them a while to grow their fur. They won't be properly fluffy until they are about a year old.

"What are you going to call them?" asked Rose.

"We don't know if they are boys or girls yet – we have to wait to go to the vet's to find out."

Sara took a picture of all the girls with the puppies to show their mums and dads and then Monisha said they should all leave Fluffikins to be alone with her newborns for a little while.

They sat in the kitchen with milk and biscuits, chatting about the puppies.

"What time is it?" asked Yasmeen.

Amber looked at the clock. "It's five to twelve — it looks as though we're having a proper midnight feast after all!"

# Chapter 10

## Fireworks and Friendship

Thursday was their last day together. The girls barely left the house apart from the occasional jump on the trampoline to burn off energy. Fluffikins wouldn't need walking for at least a couple of days while she was nursing, and the puppies provided lots of entertainment for the girls.

What with all the excitement, the

girls nearly forgot all about the Thursday night fireworks. But Amber's mum said they would go ahead as planned. Amber's siblings would help her organize them.

"We'll just make sure that Fluffikins and her pups are tucked up safely at the front of the house so that the noise doesn't bother them."

It was a clear, cold night and they all wrapped up with gloves and scarves. Monisha gave them each a sparkler, which they held at arm's length and wrote their Treasure Box initial in the blackness. *Amber, Silver, Rose and Gold.*

The garden filled with friends and neighbours of the Beau's, and Omesh,

who was training to be a chef, made some delicious spicy soup which he ladled out into mugs. They stood in the garden taking little sips.

"Now I have a cold nose but a warm tummy!" said Rose.

Sara ushered everyone towards the house so that they were a safe distance from the fireworks. Monisha began to open the boxes and get them organized.

"This reminds me of the campfire at Camp BigToes," said Yasmeen.

"Without the singing, though," said Oralie.

"And colder!" said Amber. "Oh look, there's Mrs Mack. Let's go and say hello."

Mrs Mack was wearing welly boots, rather than slippers, and a bright red bobble hat. She stood with her hands wrapped around a mug of soup.

Amber walked up first. "We really are sorry about the … misunderstanding."

Mrs Mack smiled kindly. "You were upset. Your fluffy baby was missing. I understand."

Oralie stepped forwards. "I am really the one who should say sorry. It was all my idea. Coming round to your house, I mean. Sometimes I get a bit carried away."

Mrs Mack smiled again and patted Oralie's arm. "I can get a bit carried away myself. I probably shouldn't have been feeding Snowball but she is just such a lovely dog."

Oralie thrust out a bag of tomato ketchup crisps. "I brought you these to say sorry."

Rose smiled. That was Oralie's last bag. It meant a lot from her.

Mrs Mack examined the packet before opening them and crumbling a handful on top of her soup. "Very nice, thank you," she said.

Amber smiled at Mrs Mack. "We were wondering if you would accept a gift from us too?"

"Oh, you girls! I don't need gifts. This evening is magical enough," said Mrs Mack.

"Well, it's a gift from Fluffikins, really. "We're going to keep one puppy. Like Mum said, this is such a madhouse that we'll hardly notice an extra one! But we were wondering... Would you like to have the other little puppy?"

The tears welled up in Mrs Mack's eyes.

"Oh, so kind of you, my lovely, but I couldn't take one of Snowball's babies. I go away, sometimes, you see, to visit my niece in Edinburgh. It wouldn't be fair on the poor dog."

"But Amber's family could look after it then, Mrs Mack. And it could come over the fence to see its mum and brother or sister whenever it wanted," said Rose.

Amber nodded. "They won't be old enough to leave their mum for a few weeks, but will you consider it?"

Mrs Mack passed Amber her empty soup mug and rummaged in her bag for a packet of tissues. "Maybe I will. You are lovely girls. Now make sure you stay in touch with one another. This kind of friendship doesn't come along every day." She took a tissue from the packet and walked away, dabbing at her eyes.

Amber sighed. "Mrs Mack is right.

I can't believe this half term is coming to an end and we have to go back to school! We will stay in touch, won't we?"

"Of course!" cried Rose. "Why don't we try to meet up *every* school holiday?"

All the girls nodded.

Oralie clapped her hands together. "I've already checked and Dad says you can stay at ours in the Easter holidays. You can meet *my* new puppy."

"Yay! More new puppies!" cheered the girls.

"I haven't got half as big a garden, though, and it won't be as exciting as this week."

"It will be hard to match the drama of a lost dog, a criminal investigation, a found dog and new puppies!" said Rose.

Amber put her arms around all three of her friends in a squashed-together group hug. "It doesn't matter how much room we have. Or how much drama. With friends like you, I can guarantee that whatever we do will be fun!"

At that moment, Sara started a countdown to the fireworks — "Five ... four ... three ... two ... one!!" and soon the night sky was filled with stars and showers of bright colour. The four friends stood arm-in-arm and watched.

Keep an eye out for Rose Gold and Friends: Oralie's Scavenger Hunt

# Chapter 1

## A Barking Beige Bundle

Amber, Yasmeen and Rose couldn't have been more excited. It was nearly two months since they had seen one another. Now it was the Easter holidays and they were getting together at Oralie's house.

Rose's mum dropped them off. Oralie's house was a neat semi-detached with a black front door and a birdbath in the front garden. Rose's mum parked the car on the driveway and the girls jumped out. They rushed to knock at the front door and Oralie appeared from behind the curtains in the front window, waving madly. Then she disappeared, presumably to come and let them in. A high yapping sound came from behind the front door.

"That must be Sampson," said Yasmeen. Sampson was Oralie's new puppy.

"I can't wait to meet him," said Rose. She didn't have to wait long. Oralie opened the door and hugged the girls tight.

As soon as the door was closed, Oralie's dad opened the crate in the kitchen. A small beige, barking bundle shot out as if he'd been projected. He zoomed along the floor, little legs struggling on the shiny tiles. He ran in yapping circles around their legs and then sat on Oralie's feet. She scooped him into her arms and held him so that his four paws were pointing forwards.

"This is Sampson," she said, with a wide grin. "He goes in his crate every night or if he's getting overexcited. It's his safe space but he still loves to come out!"

# Look out for the other Rose Gold books...

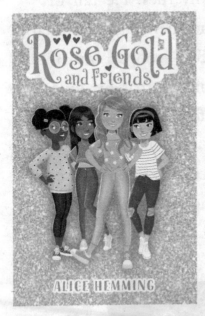

Yasmeen's Winter Fun

ALICE HEMMING

Oralie's Scavenger Hunt

ALICE HEMMING